Thirty Letters

Various Subjects

Vol. 1

William Jackson

Alpha Editions

This edition published in 2023

ISBN : 9789357949095

Design and Setting By
Alpha Editions
www.alphaedis.com
Email - info@alphaedis.com

Contents

VOL. 1

LETTER I.

SINCE you request that our correspondence should be out of the beaten track, be it so. My retirement from the world will naturally give an air of peculiarity to my sentiments, which perhaps may entertain where it does not convince. In justice to myself, let me observe, that truth sometimes does not strike us without the assistance of custom; but so great is the force of custom, that, unassisted by truth, it has worked the greatest miracles. Need I bring for proof the quantity of nonsense in all the arts, sciences, and even religion itself, which it has sanctified? As possibly in the course of my letters to you I may attack some received doctrines on each of these subjects, let not what I advance be instantly rejected, because contrary to an opinion founded on prejudice; but, as much as possible, divest yourself of the partiality acquired by habit, and if at last you should not agree with me, I shall suspect my sentiments to be peculiar and not just.

Tho' truth may want the assistance of use before we feel its force, yet when it is really felt, we detest what custom only made us like. The difficulty is to procure for truth a fair examination. The multitude is always against it. The first discovery in any thing is considered as an encroachment upon property, a property become sacred by possession. Discoverers are accordingly treated as criminals, and must have good luck to escape execution.

I mean not to rank myself with such bold adventurers; I am neither ambitious of the honour, or the danger, of enlightening the world, but, if I can soften prejudices which I cannot remove—if I can loosen the fetters of custom where I cannot altogether unbind them, and engage you to think for yourself—my end will be answered, and my trouble fully repaid.

Adieu! &c.

LETTER II.

IT is natural to suppose, that people originally judged of things by their senses and immediate perceptions. By degrees they found that their senses were not infallible, and that things frequently contradicted their first appearance. This, at last, was pushed to an extravagance; and certain philosophers endeavoured to persuade mankind, that the senses deceive us so often, that we can never depend on them—that we cannot tell whether we are in motion or at rest, asleep or awake, with many other such absurdities. They used the same ingenuity with the mental sense. Some ancient sage was asked, "Who is the richest man?" if he had replied "He that has most money," the answer would have been natural and just—what he did say, every one knows. We have suffered ourselves to be imposed on so long, that at last we begin to impose on ourselves.

Riches, cards, and duelling, have been constantly abused, written, and preached against; and yet men will still hoard, play, and fight. Why should they? All universal passions we may fairly pronounce to be natural, and should be treated with respect. The gratification of our passions are our greatest pleasures, and he that has most gratifications is of course the happiest man. This, as a general assertion, is true, and it is true also in particulars, provided we pay no more for pleasure than it is worth.

Every man should endeavour to be rich. He that has money may possess every thing that is transferable—this is a sufficient inducement to procure it. Nay, if he possesses nothing but his money, if he considers it as the end, as well as the means, it is still right to be rich: for, knowing that he has it in his power to procure every thing, he is as well satisfied as is the thing itself was in his possession. This is the true source of the miser's pleasure; and a great pleasure it is! A moral philosopher may tell him, "that man does not live for himself alone, and that he hurts the community by withholding what would be of use to it"—this he thinks to be weak reasoning. The sneers of wits signify as little; for he knows they would be glad to be rich if they could. He feels that the pleasure arising from the possession of riches, whether used or not, is too great to be given up for all the wit, or even the strongest arguments that can be brought against it.

It seems to be agreed, that card-playing proceeds entirely from avarice—tho' this may sometimes be the motive, yet it may with more probability be derived from other, and more general principles.

The mind of man naturally requires employment, and that employment is most agreeable, which engages, without fatiguing the attention. There is nothing for this purpose of such universal attraction as cards. The fine arts and belles lettres can only be enjoyed by those who have a genius for them—

other studies and amusements have their particular charm, but cards are the universal amusement in every country where they are known. The alternate changes in the play, the hope upon the taking up a new hand, and the triumph of getting a game, made more compleat from the fear of losing it, keep the mind in a perpetual agitation, which is found by experience to be too agreeable to be quitted for any other consideration. The stake played for is a quickener of these sensations, but not the cause. Children who play for nothing feel what I have been describing perhaps in a more exquisite degree than he who engages for thousands. A state of inaction is of all others the most dreadful! and it is to avoid this inaction that we seek employment, though at the expence of health, temper, and fortune. This subject is finely touched by Abbé du Bos, in his reflexions upon poetry, &c. indeed he carries it so far as to say, that the pleasure arising from an extraordinary agitation of the mind, is frequently so great as to stifle humanity; and from hence arises the entertainment of the common people at executions, and of the better sort at tragedies. Tho' in this last instance he may be mistaken; yet, the delight we feel in reading the actions of a hero may be referred to this cause. The moralist censures the taste of those who can be pleased with the actions of an Alexander or a Nadir Shah—the Truth is, we do not approve the actions; but the relation of them causes that agitation of the mind which we find to be pleasant. The reign of Henry the seventh, tho' of the greatest consequence to this nation, does not interest us like the contentions of York and Lancaster by which the kingdom was ruined.—It is in vain that we are told that scenes of war and bloodshed can give no pleasure to a good mind, and that the true hero is he who cultivates the arts of peace, he by whom men are benefited not he by whom they are destroyed—it is to no purpose—we sleep over the actions of quiet goodness, while aspiring, destroying greatness, claims and commands our attention.

Duelling has in many countries a law against it—but can never be prevented. The law can inflict no greater penalty for any breach of it than death; which the duellist contemns.—There are also some cases of injury which the law cannot prevent, nor punish when committed—these must be redressed by the man who suffers, and by him *only*. He is prompted to do this by something antecedent, and superior to all law, and by a desire as eager as hunger or lust; so that it is as easy for law to prevent or restrain the two latter as the former. Very luckily for us, occasions for the gratifications of this passion occur but seldom: and tho' a man may be restrained from a duel by personal fear, which is its only counteractor, there are very few instances, perhaps none, of its being prevented by considering it so a breach of the law. In the beginning of the last century duels were as frequent, particularly in France, as to occasion a severe edict to prevent them—indeed by their frequency, they were by degrees improved into combats of two, three, and sometimes more of a side.—In those days a French nobleman was making up his party to decide a quarrel with another man of equal rank, it came to the King's ears, who sent to him one of the most rising men at court with a command to desist, assuring him of the strict execution of the edict in case of disobedience.—Every one knows the attachment of the French to their sovereign, but yet it proved weak when set against this all-powerful passion. The nobleman not only refused to obey the king, but actually engaged the messenger to be one of his party.

The above seem to be the principal reasons why riches, cards, and duelling have so deep a root in the mind of man—but there are others which come in aid. The desire of superiority is of itself almost sufficient to produce this great effect.

Believe me ever yours, &c.

LETTER III.

I Cannot comply with your desire—a regular dissertation is above me——but if you will take my thoughts as they occur, the honour of methodizing them shall be yours.

Languages are termed rough and smooth, weak or expressive, frequently without reason.—As these are comparative terms, they change their application according to circumstances. The French is said to be a smooth or rough language, when compared with the German or Italian. Perhaps this is true, and yet we should not determine too hastily. In appearance, there are more vowels in the Italian language than in the French; but in pronunciation the French lose many Consonants, and the Italians none: and yet in French, so great is the irregularity of that language, many consonants are pronounced which are not written——smoothness or roughness must therefore depend on the ear alone, yet how far a Language is weak or expressive, may be treated of and determined with precision.

Every sentence may be considered as the picture of an idea; the quicker that picture is presented to the mind, the stronger is its Impression. That language then which is shortest, is the most expressive. If we should fix on any language as being in general the most concise, yet, if in some instances it is more diffuse than another, then, in those instances the latter is most expressive. This, I believe, is an universal rule, and without exception.

Let us for the present suppose Latin to be more expressive, because shorter, than any modern language, and compare it with English in some examples, just as they occur. *Captus oculis* and *cæcus*—are used for the same thing—the last is more expressive than the first, and both less so than blind: a single syllable does the office of many. How much more forcibly does it strike us to be told that our friend is dead, than *mortuus est*, or *Mors continuo ipsum occupavit?* This last is indeed poetical, if we suppose death a person. Tho' I just now said that Latin was closer in its expression than any modern language, it was only in compliance with common opinion; for I have great reason to believe that it yields in this respect to English: The latin hexameter and Terence's line being with ease included in our heroic verse, which is not so long by many syllables. There have been many pieces of English poetry translated into Latin, and, in general nothing can read more dead and unanimated. In the eighth volume of the Spectator is a translation of the famous soliloquy in the Play of Cato—compare it with the original, and observe how the same thought is strong in English and weak in Latin, occasioned entirely by its being close in one language, and diffuse in the other: for, as much as one sentence exceeds another in length, in the same proportion does it fail in expression.

Translations, most commonly, are more verbose than their original, which is one reason for their weakness; whenever they are less so, they are stronger. Suppose we should find in a French author these phrases, *Un Canon de neuf livres de Balle—Un Vaisseau du Roi du quatre vingt dix Pieces du Canon*; and they were rendered into English by *a nine-pounder—A ninety-gun ship*—is not the translation more spirited than the original? I purposely chose a phrase with as little matter in it as possible, where the meaning could not be mistaken, and in which there was no variety of expression, that the trial might be fairer. I have heard that the German is an expressive language—it may be so, I do not understand it; but I can perceive that, for the most part, the words are very long, which makes against its being so. French, and Italian particularly, are much more diffuse than English. Translations from these languages have often a force that the originals wanted; and this not owing to the English being a stronger language in *sound*, as some have imagined, but to strength occasioned by brevity.

Perhaps it may be imagined, that those words which carry their signification with them should be most expressive, whether long or short; that is, when they are derived from, or compounded of known words, which express that signification. But this is not so. When we say *adieu, farewell*—we mean no more than a ceremony at parting.—No one considers *adieu* as a recommendation to God, or *farewell* as a wish for happiness.—Frequent use destroys all idea of derivation. But if we speak a compound or self-significative word that is not common, we perceive the derivation of it. Thus if a Londoner says *butter-milk*, he has an idea of something compounded of butter and milk; but to an Irishman or Hollander, it is as simple an idea as either of the words taken separately, is to us.

It is but late that our orthography was fixed even in the most common words. Two hundred years ago, every person spelt as he liked: a privilege enjoyed still later than that period by "royal and noble authors," who seem, in this instance, to claim the liberty enjoyed by their ancestors. Since the time orthography has been thought of some consequence, we have attended partly to pronunciation, tho' chiefly to derivation. But, in some cases, where we should altogether have spelt according to derivation, we have taken pronunciation for our guide. And this has occasioned some confusion; for instance *naught* is *bad*—*nought* is *nothing*; these terms were long confounded, and even now are not kept perfectly distinct, which has occasioned *ought* to be written *aught*. *Wrapt* is envelloped—*rapt* is hurried away, or totally possessed: the first of these is frequently used for the last, by some of our modern poets. *Marry* is an asseveration—*marry*, to give in marriage—the spelling these words the same, confounds them together; we should have preserved for the first, the real word *mary*. It was a common thing formerly to swear by *Mary*, the *a* in which was pronounced broad, as the Priests of that time did the Latin *Maria*, from whom the common people took the pronunciation. In one of the pieces in the first volume of the collection of old plays, it frequently occurs, and is spelt as a proper name, *Marie*. Permit me to observe, that the Editor, by modernizing the spelling in the other volumes, has prevented their being made this use of, as they might have shewed the progress of orthography as well as of dramatic poetry.

In the reign of James the first were many attempts to reduce orthography altogether to pronunciation. In our time we have seen some attempts to bring it altogether from derivation—but surely both were wrong. Whoever reads Howel's letters, or Dr. Newton's Milton, will see, that by a partial principle too generally adopted, they have made of the English language "a very fantastical banquet—just so many strange dishes!"

There are many inversions of phrases used in poetry which are contrary to the genius of our language. In the translation of the Iliad there frequently occurs "thunders the sky"——"totters the ground," meaning that "the sky thunders" and "the ground totters." This change of position has the authority of some of our best poets, tho' it frequently obscures the sense, and sometimes makes it directly contrary to what is intended to be expressed. Our language does not, with ease, admit of the nominative after the verb. If we read, tho' in poetry, "shakes the ground" we do not readily understand that "the ground shakes," but rather refer to some antecedent nominative that has produced this effect. To adopt the construction of the ancient languages is as awkward as to adopt their measures. You will understand this to be meant as a general observation, the truth of which is not destroyed by a few exceptions where the inversion may be happily used. The sense in these verses of Pope "halts" as much by Roman construction, as the Rhythmus in Sidney does by "Roman feet."

In reading Latin and Greek we are obliged to keep the sense suspended until we come to the end of the period, but it is not so in any modern language that I know of, except now and then in Italian poetry; so that there is a sameness of construction in all of them when compared with the ancient languages. Now, this suspension of the sense is surely no advantage, therefore if it were possible to make English like Latin and Greek in this respect, it would hurt the language.

In another letter I may possibly resume this subject.

I am, &c.

LETTER IV.

OUR greatest mistake in the pursuit of happiness as well as of science, is to judge by the perceptions of others, and not by our own. This perversion is admirably ridiculed in some comedy, in which a young fellow naturally sober, gives into debaucheries merely because they are fashionable. "I am horrid sick"—says he—"I am tired to death—I hate cards—but it is *life* for all that!"

My friend, examine your heart—You yourself are the best judge of what contributes to your own happiness. Is the pleasure of shooting equal to the fatigue?... Put down the gun. Is the cry of the hounds a sufficient charm to remove the fear of breaking your neck?... Come off your horse.—And in pure charity let me advise the "*im*patient fisher" to convert his rod into a walking stick, jemmy, and switch. "For what? Do not gentlemen love country diversions?" But if *you* do not, why should you be governed by *their* inclinations?

Mr. Connoisseur, do not pretend raptures at music, you know you have no ear.—Stare not at that picture, you are sensible you have no eye.—Close that book, let others weep; you have no heart. "Sir, it is the taste to admire music, painting, and fine writing."—I am very glad of it.—But it is not *your* taste, here

―――――――hinc Vos,

Vos hinc, mutatis discedite partibus—

Now confess honestly Mr. Sportsman, that you have more pleasure in Snyder's pictures, than from hunting in propriâ personâ—that the French horns at a concert have more harmony than in a wood. And, Mr. Connoisseur, you are now in your element.—Is it not better to "join the jovial chace" than the insipid crew of the dilettanti?

Let us remember and practice the old maxim.

―――――――trahit *sua* quemque Voluptas.

―――――――――――――――――

LETTER V.

Dear Sir,

I Am glad you go on with your painting. Though you should never arrive at any great degree of excellence yourself, it will infallibly make you a better judge of the excellencies of others. You tell me, what indeed every Connoisseur says by rote, that the great painters painted above, beyond nature! That they painted beyond nature I grant, but not above, if by above we are to understand something more excellent than what we find in nature. I have long been sick of the cant of writers and talkers upon this subject. If it be possible, let us speak a little common-sense—endeavour to shew what seems by our feelings to be the truth, and then prevent a wrong application of it.

The great painters, it is agreed, painted beyond nature—but how? Why, if I may venture to say it, by drawing and colouring extravagantly. But were they right or wrong in doing so? This depends upon circumstances. I remember seeing at a Painter's a head taken from nature, another copied from Hans Holbein, and a third from Giulio Romano—upon which the artist made a dissertation.—He first produced the portrait from nature, and asked me how I liked it? I told him that there appeared to me great simplicity and elegance in it, and an excellence which I thought essential to a good picture—a proper ballance between the light and shade of every part. (I meant that the shade of the white was lighter than that of blue—of blue fainter than of black, &c. so that each colour was as perceivable in the shadows as lights.) Ay, says he, that is true, but I will shew you a style preferable to it—Upon which he produced the copy from Holbein.—I agreed, that it was stronger, and such as nature might appear in many instances.——But here, says he, is something *beyond* nature; this I call the sublime style of painting, and this I will try to bring my heads to.—Then he discovered the copy from Giulio— there is strength, says he—see how faint the others are.—Now, acknowledge that the picture I painted from nature is nothing to it. It must be confessed, I replied, that the extravagance of the last picture does for a moment dazzle our eyes—yours seems weak by the comparison, it is like looking upon white paper after staring at the sun.—On the contrary, if I pass from yours to this, I am hurt at seeing every thing so extravagant, and so far *beyond the modesty of nature!*—"It is not intended to be strictly natural, it is the *fine ideal*, it is something above, beyond nature!" "I must own that I have no idea of any beauty beyond what may be found in nature—indeed, whence is the idea to be taken? But do not think I rate Giulio or any of the sublime painters lightly; I am so sensible of their merit, that, contrary perhaps to your expectation, I am about to defend their practice. They generally painted for churches, where the picture is seen in a bad light, or at a distance; so that it could not be seen at all if the manner was not violent: both the drawing and colouring must be extravagant to strike—for which reason, they overcharged their attitudes, blackened their shadows, reddened their carnations, and whitened their lights; and all this with the greatest propriety. But if you apply this practice to closet or portrait painting, what is an excellence in them, becomes a defect in you. This picture which you have copied with so much success, I dare say has an admirable effect where it hangs; but near the eye or in a strong light, it is hard and over-done. On the other hand, if your portrait was to be hung at a great distance, or in an obscure place, the delicate touches I now admire would escape the sight. The style proper for the church is improper for the closet, and the contrary. The great painters were in the right then, in painting *beyond nature*; but let us not imagine that such figures and characters are therefore the most beautiful. No painter can invent a figure surpassing the *finest* of nature: for character and form, nature is the *just* and *only* standard. He shews his genius more by properly associating natural objects, and expressing natural characters, than by exaggerating them or by inventing new ones."

When I receive the picture you have promised me, I will criticise it with as much sincerity as

I am your Friend, &c.

LETTER VI.

YOU have turned my thoughts much towards painting of late—I have been trying to solve this question.

What is the reason that those objects which displease us, or at best, that pass unnoticed, in nature, please us most in painting?

A deep road, a puddle of water, a bank covered with docks and briars, and an old tree or two, are all the circumstances in many a fine landscape. As clowns and half starved cattle are the figures a landscape-painter chuses for his pictures; so, rough-looking fellows wrapt up in sheets and blankets, are chosen by the history-painter, to express the greatest personages, and in the most dignified actions of their lives.

Let the following observations have what weight they may—tho' they do not clearly answer, they seem to throw some light on this difficult question.

1. While we are uncultivated, like the Irish Oscar, if we are to be awakened, it must be by having a great stone thrown against our heads. The man of the utmost elegance and refinement may remember the time when, in reading, nothing moved him but the marvellous, and in painting, nothing pleased him but the glaring. While he was in this state, he delighted in books of chivalry and Chinese pictures—these gave place to less extravagant representations of life; and at last by much converse with men of taste, reading purer authors, and seeing better pictures, he is taught how to feel, and finds a perfect revolution even in his sensations. Those objects which once delighted him, he now despises—these, on the contrary, he formerly took no notice of, he now sees with rapture; and even goes so far as to admire the objects in nature, *he has learnt* to like in representation.—Now, it is this improved, tho' artificial state of the mind that constitutes the judge of painting—and it is the judge the painter is sollicitous to please.—He is to attain this end then, by departing as much as possible from what is our natural barbarous taste, and by conforming to that we have acquired.

2. It is most certain that in all the arts we make difficulties in order to shew our skill in conquering them.—Some French writer calls this principle *la difficultè vaincue*; and this conquest is the source of much pleasure. What is it but this that induces the novellist and play-writer to embarrass their characters with difficulties and troubles? What is there but this that can make a musical canon to be thought fine in composition, or extravagant execution in performance agreeable, when the mind cannot comprehend the one, nor the ear follow the other? and, to bring it to the present subject—what is it but this that induces the painter to make use of the most unpromising objects, and produce beauty where you might expect nothing but deformity?

3. It is necessary that a painter should chuse such objects as are capable of variety either from shape or arrangement. Regular formal objects admit but little, especially those where art has the greatest share in their production, unless they are capable of motion, as ships, windmills, &c. and then they become pictoresque by a proper choice of attitude. It is curious to observe the shifts to which artists are reduced, when they are obliged to paint such objects as are in themselves unpictoresque—suppose a fine house with avenues of trees. They will vary the tint of the stones in the one, and of the leaves in the other, or by throwing in accidental shades and lights produce a variety. In like manner, portrait-painters undress the hair, loosen the coat, and wrinkle the stockings that they may produce a variety in the *manner* of *treating* a subject which wanted it in form.

Those objects which have no set form have of course most variety. A road or river may wind in any direction—trees are of all sizes and shapes, may stand here or there—loose drapery admits of a thousand folds and dispositions which the stiff modern dress is incapable of. So that the painter by taking these has ample materials for shewing his judgment in form, or skill in arrangement——for making, and overcoming difficulties—and lastly, by the uniting both these he conforms to the principles by which the cultivated taste is pleased—the ultimate end of all the fine arts.

If you are not satisfied with this solution, help me to a better—but give a fair reading to this of

Your sincere friend, &c.

LETTER **VII.**

I Do not admit your excuse.—A genius should never comply with *local* or *temporary* taste—instead of debasing himself to the people, he should elevate the people to him. When Milton subtilizes divinity, and Shakespeare "cracks the wind of a poor phrase;" who but wishes that those great poets had not descended from their sphere?

Your allusions to incidents which must soon be forgot, are only worthy of a writer who expects but a short existence. It is true our plays abound with such allusions. When Foigard, in the Beaux Stratagem, says he is a subject of the King of Spain—they ask him in a fury "which King of Spain?" This did very well at the time; but these two Kings of Spain are now of much less consequence than their brother monarchs of Brentford. I think it is in the same play where one of the characters is asked "when he was at church last?" he should answer "at the coronation;" but it is a point to give a reply that shall suit the time when the play is performed, forgetting that there are many expressions which remove you back into the last century when the play was written. I remember in the late King's reign the reply used to be "at the installation;" at the accession of his present Majesty an actor thought he had a good opportunity of returning to "coronation," but unluckily it was before the King was crowned.

Allusions of this sort soon become obscure, and yet they will not bear being altered. "Pray you avoid them."

Adieu, &c.

LETTER VIII.

TRUE, my friend, musicians do commit strange absurdities by way of expression—but fanciful people make them commit others which they never thought of.

The most common mistake of composers is to express words and not ideas. This is generally the case with Purcel, and frequently with Handel. I believe there is not a single piece existing of the former, if it has a word to be played upon, but will prove my assertion: and the latter, if the impetuosity of the musical subject will give him leave, will at any time quit it for a pun. There is no trap so likely to catch composers as the words *high* and *low*, *down* and *up*. "By G— (as Quin says) they must bite." In what raptures was Purcel when he set "They that *go down* to the sea in ships." How lucky a circumstance, that there was a singer at that time, who could *go down* to DD, and *go up* two Octaves above? for there is in other parts of the anthem a going *up* as well as *down*. The whole is a constellation of beauties of this kind. Handel had leisure, at the conclusion of an excellent movement, to endeavour at an imitation of the rocking of a cradle (See the end of the anthem "My heart is inditing"), and has his *ups* and *downs* too in plenty. If many examples of this may be found in these great geniuses, it would be endless to enumerate the instances in those of the lower order. Let it suffice to observe, that all operas without exception, the greatest part of church-music, and particularly Marcello's psalms, abound in this ridiculous imitative expression.

This is trifling with the words and neglecting the sentiment; but the fault is much increased when a word is expressed in contradiction to the sentiment. A most flagrant instance of this is in Boyce's Solomon, in the song of "Arise my Fair One come away."—The hero of the piece is inviting his mistress to come to him, and to tempt her the more, in describing the beauty of the spring, he tells her that

"Stern winter's *gone* with all its train

"Of chilling frosts and dropping rain,"

but it is *come* in the music—the unlucky words of *winter*, *frost*, and *rain*, made the composer set the lover a shivering, when he was full of the feelings of the "genial ray!"

But sometimes expression of the sentiment is blameable, if such expression is improper for the general subject of the piece. Religious solemnity should not appear at the theatre, nor theatrical levity at the church. In the *Stabat Mater* of Pergolesi, and in the *Messiah* of Handel, there is an expression of whipping attempted, which, if it is understood at all, conveys either a ludicrous or prophane idea, according to the disposition of the hearer. Permit me to suspend my subject a moment just to observe, that there is sometimes mention made in plays, of providence, God, and other subjects, which are as incompatible with a place of public entertainment, as the common sentiments of plays are with the church. If we are disgusted at a theatrical preacher, we are not less offended when an actor heightens all these ill-placed sentiments—forcing them upon your notice by an affectation of a deep sense of religion, and most solemnly preaching the sermon which the poet so improperly wrote.

All these, and many more, are faults which musicians *really* commit; but a connoisseur will make them guilty of others, by way of compliment, which the composers never dreamt of. The introduction of the Coronation anthem, *Zadok the Priest*, is an arpeggio, which Handel probably took from his own performance at the harpsichord; but a great judge says, it is to express the murmurs of the people assembled in the abbey. "All we like sheep are gone astray" in the Messiah is considered as most excellently expressing the breaking out of sheep from a field.—— But out of pity to the connoisseurs, virtuosi, and the most respectable *Conoscenti*, I will not increase my instances—God forbid I should rob any man of his criticism!

Lest I should encroach upon *your* premises, I will quit such dangerous ground, and leave you with more celerity than ceremony.

LETTER IX.

I Like every part of your poem except the parenthesis towards the conclusion. In the midst of a rapid description, or tender sentiment; or any thing that commands the attention, or attaches the heart; what is more disgustful than to have the image cut in two, for the sake of explaining a word, or removing an objection, which the reader may possibly make?

Milton and Shakespeare frequently interrupt the most lively and ardent passages—take some instances as they occur.

Their arms away they threw, and to the hills

(For earth hath this variety from heav'n

Of pleasure situate in hill or dale)

Light as the lightning's glimpse they ran, they flew.

PAR. LOST. B. VI.

————when on a day

(For time, though in eternity, apply'd

To motion, measures all things durable

By present, past, and future) on such a day

As heaven's great year brings forth.

PAR. LOST. B. V.

————evening now approach'd

(For we have also our evening and our morn,

We ours for change delectable, not need)

Forthwith from dance to sweet repast they turn

Desirous; &c.

Upon the mention of *hills* in the first quotation, and of *day* and *evening* in the second and last—he knew that he had some objections to answer, and accordingly set about doing it for fear of the consequences—I wish they had remained in their full force.

You have often read the Midsummer Night's Dream—do you recollect this passage?

Lys. *Hermia*, for ought that ever I could read,

Could ever hear by tale or history,
The course of true love never did run smooth;
But, either it was different in blood——

Her. O cross! too high, to be enthrall'd to low!——

Lys. Or else misgrafted in respect of years—

Her. O spite! too old, to be engag'd to young!

Lys. Or else it stood upon the choice of friends—

Her. O hell! to chuse love by another's eye!

Lys. Or if there were a sympathy in choice—

War, death, or sickness did lay siege to it.

Read it without Hermia's interruptions and it becomes one of the finest parts of the author—but it is miserably mangled as it stands.

You will remember that it is the improper use of the parenthesis I object to and not to the thing itself. "This figure of composition," says a late ingenious author, "which is hardly ever used in common discourse, is much employed by the best writers of antiquity, in order to give a cast and colour to their style different from common idiom, and by Demosthenes particularly; and not only by the orators, but the poets."

I would recommend to your consideration whether you had not better avoid giving any hint how the story of your poem is to conclude? Anticipation frequently spoils a fine incident. When Æneas is reciting to Dido what past at Troy, says he,

Arduus armatos mediis in mænibus astans

Fundit equus.

ÆN. II.

The first mention of the Horse's having armed men within, should have been reserved for this place. There is something truly terrible and sublime in Æneas's being waked by such a variety of horrid sounds, and ignorant of the cause; the reader also should have been ignorant until Pantheus explained the mystery. See the whole passage in Æn. II. beginning at the 298th verse, and if possible, forget that this went before.

Delecta virum fortiti corpora furtim

Includunt cæco lateri, &c.

One of the finest parts of Don Quixote is also spoiled by mentioning a circumstance which should have been delayed. The Knight and his 'Squire, at the close of the day, hear the clank of chains, and dreadful blows, which would have puzzled the reader as much as it frightened them, had not the author unluckily said "that the strokes were in *time* and *measure*," which is telling us very plainly that it was a mill. The whole scene is highly pictoresque and beautiful.

If these hints will be of any service to you it will be a great pleasure to

Yours, &c.

LETTER **X.**

THE productions of genius require some ages to be brought to perfection. The liberal arts have their infancy, youth and manhood; and, to carry on the allusion, continue sometime in a state of strength, and then verge by degrees to a decline, which at last ends in a total extinction. The English language, poetry, and music, exhibit proofs of this observation, as far as they have as yet gone: with the two former I have at present nothing to do, but shall confine what I have to say on this subject to the latter.

What the music of the times preceding Harry the eighth was, I confess myself ignorant, nor indeed is the knowledge of it necessary: we may conclude that it was more barbarous than that of the sixteenth century, as the times in which it was used were less enlightened. Some masses, mottets, and madrigals are what have reached us. The whole consists of a succession of chords without art or meaning, and perfectly destitute of air. In Elizabeth's reign appeared some composers, Tallis, Bird, Morley, and Farrant, which improved the barren style of their predecessors: they had more choice in their harmony, and made some little advances in melody. There are some pieces of instrumental music composed at this time which still exist: particularly a book of lessons, for the virginals, which was the Queen's.—Whether the composers thought that her sacred Majesty excelled in musical abilities as much as in rank, or as she wished to do in beauty, I know not; but this is certain, that these pieces are so crowded with parts, and so aukwardly barbarous, as to render the performance of them impossible—so natural is it, even in the infancy of art, to mistake difficulty for beauty.

I do not recollect any composer that really improved music for the first half of the seventeenth century, except Orlando Gibbons; of whom, a service for the church, and two or three anthems remain, the harmony of which is good, and the melody pleasing. In the Gloria Patri of the Nunc Dimittis is the best canon, in my judgment, that was ever made. Gibbons was also a composer for the virginals, but in no respect better than his predecessors. I believe it was about this time that the species of canon called the catch, was produced. The intent of my making this short recapitulation of the former state of music is purely prefatory to what I have to say upon the subject of catches.

This odd species of composition, whenever invented, was brought to its perfection by Purcel. Real music was as yet in its childhood; but the reign of Charles the second carried every kind of vulgar debauchery to its height. The proper æra for the birth of such pieces as "when quartered, have ever three parts obscenity, and one part music."

The definition of a catch is a piece for three or more voices, one of which leads, and the others follow in the same notes. It must be so contrived, that rests (which are made for that purpose) in the music of one line be filled up with a word or two from another line; these form a cross-purpose or catch, from whence the name. Now, this piece of wit is not judged perfect, if the result be not the rankest indecency.

Perhaps this definition may be objected to, and I may be told that there are catches perfectly harmless. It is true that some pieces are called catches that have nothing to offend, and others that may justly pretend to please; but they want what is absolutely necessary for a catch—the break, and cross-purpose.

It may also be said that the result of the break, is not always indecency. I confess there are catches upon other subjects, drunkenness is a favourite one; which, though good, is not so *very* good as the other: and there may possibly be found one or two upon other topicks which might be heard without disgust; but these are not sufficient to contradict a general rule, or make me retract what I have advanced.

I will next examine their musical merit.—And this as compositions must consist either in their harmony, or melody; or their effect in performance.

The harmony of a catch is nothing more than the common result of filling up a chord.—There is not contrivance enough to make it esteemed as a piece of ingenuity. "What! they are all canons!" So is every tune in the world, if you will set it in three or more parts, and sing those parts in succession as a catch—but a *real* canon is not so easily produced: it is one of those difficult trifles which costs an infinite deal of labour, and after all is worth nothing. I do not except the famous *Non nobis* of Bird, in which are some passages not to be endured. The excellence in the composition of a catch consists in making the breaks, and filling them up properly. The melody is, for the most part, the unimproved vulgar drawl of the times of ignorance.

Let us next attend to the manner of performance. One voice leads, a second follows, and a third, &c. succeeds, unaccompanied with any instrument to keep them in tune together. The consequence is, that the voices are always sinking, but not equally, for the best singer will keep nearest the pitch, and the others depart farthest from it. If the parts are doubled, which is sometimes the case, all these defects are multiplied. To this let there be added the imperfect scale of an uncultivated voice, the *departing* from the real sound by way of humour, the noise of so many people striving to outsing each other, the confusion of speaking different words at the same time, and all this heightened by the laughing and other accompaniments of the audience—it presents such a scene of savage folly as would not disgrace the Hottentots indeed, but is not much to the credit of a company of civilized people.

As the catch in a manner owed its existence to a drunken club, of which some musicians were members; upon their dying, it languished for years, and was scarce known except among choir-men, who now and then kept up the spirit of their forefathers. As the age grew more polished, a better style of music appeared. Corelli gave a new turn to instrumental music, and was successfully followed by Geminiani and Handel; the last excelled in vocal as well as instrumental music.

There have been refinements and confessed improvements upon all these great men since; and no doubt but at this time there are much better performers, and more elegant, tho' less solid composers. This is the united effect of the labours of the whole together, for there is no *one man* to be compared with either of the above-mentioned.

Now, if this were speculation only, is it credible that taste should revert to barbarism? Its natural death is, to be frittered away in false refinement; and yet, contrary to experience in every other instance, we have gone back a century, and catches flourish in the reign of George the third. There is a club composed of some of the first people in the kingdom which meet professedly to hear this species of composition: they cultivate it and encourage it with premiums. To obtain which, many composers, who ought to be above such nonsense, become candidates, and produce such things

——"one knows not what to call,

"Their generation's so equivocal."

Sometimes a piece makes its appearance that was lately found by accident after a concealment of a hundred and fifty years. When it is approved, and declared too excellent for these degenerate days, the author smiles and owns it. I scarce ever saw one of these things that did not betray itself, within three bars, to be modern. It is as difficult to imitate ancient music as ancient poetry; a few square notes are not sufficient for the one, nor will two or three *whiloms* and *ekes* do for the other. And yet in this last instance a few affected antiquated spellings have been thought by one half of the world, sufficient to weigh against modern phraseology, modern manners, and even modern facts. Surely it requires no great discernment to discover that what has existed may be imitated, but nothing less than the gift of Prescience can dive into futurity. If it is *improbable* that an uneducated boy should be able to produce what are called Rowley's Poems, it is *impossible* that Rowley could write in a style and allude to facts of after times. Forgive me this digression, but indeed I have nearly finished my subject and letter.

I profess that I never heard a catch sung, but I felt more ashamed than I can express. I pretend to no more delicacy than that of the age I live in, which is very properly too refined to endure such barbarisms—I was ashamed for myself—for my company—and if a foreigner was present—for my country.

It has just occurred to me that you like catches, and frequently help to sing them—revenge yourself for the liberties I have taken, by compelling me to hear some of these pleasant ditties, when perhaps I may be forced to sing in my own defence.

Adieu.

P. S. If you should have a design to convert me—take me to the catch-club.—I confess, and honour, the superior excellence of its performance, while I lament that so noble a subscription should be lavished for so poor a purpose as keeping alive musical false-wit, when it might so powerfully support and encourage the best style of composition; and rather advance our taste by anticipating the improvements of the coming age, than force it back to times of barbarism, from which it has cost us such pains to emerge.

LETTER XI.

I Know that you are one of those who consider our language as past its meridian. Some think it was in its highest lustre in the age of Sidney; others, in that of Addison. Perhaps, upon an impartial review of it, we shall find it more perfect now than ever.

In the authors before the reign of Elizabeth, there seems not the least pretence to a simple, natural style. A man was held unfit to write, who could not express his thoughts out of the common language; so that it is possible, there was as much difficulty in understanding them at the time they lived, as now. If we are to judge of the English they spoke, by that they writ, we have no reason to complain of the fluctuation of our tongue. But it is very probable that conversation-language was much the same two hundred years ago as at present; there are proofs of this in private letters still existing—I mean from such people as had no ambition to be thought learned, or from such as felt too much for affectation. The famous letter of Ann Boleyn to Henry the eighth, is of this last sort, in which there is scarce an obsolete expression.——I hope you make a distinction between expression and spelling—for as I once observed to you, it is but of late that our orthography has been fixed. In the State-tryals in Elizabeth and James's reign, we find near the same language we use at present, and this was taken immediately from the mouth. In those passages where Shakespeare's genius had not its full scope, may be observed his attempts to be thought learned, and refined; but where the subject was too impetuous to brook restraint, the language is as perfect as the idea. Upon the whole, tho' the colloquial English was much the same as at present, we may safely pronounce the style of the *authors* of this period to be barbarous.

 The disputes between Charles the first and the Parliament, were of great use in polishing the language; and tho' the King's papers are thought to be most elegant, yet it is evident that both parties endeavoured at strength for the good of their cause, and at perspicuity for the sake of being universally understood—and these two principles go near towards making a perfect style. Milton's prose is in general very nervous, but it is not free from stiffness and affectation.

The other period is that of Addison. He was undoubtedly one of our smoothest and best writers: he had the skill of uniting ease, strength, and correctness, and did more towards improving the language than the united labours of fifty years before him. But yet there were some little remains of barbarism still left, which are evident enough in his contemporaries, and may be discovered even in him, by attending to the style and not to the matter.

Will you believe that so elegant a writer has used *authenticalness* for *authenticity*?——You may find this horrid word in his Dialogues on Medals.

Political disputes have produced, among many bad effects, the same good, now, as formerly—they have improved our language. Those in the Administration of Sir Robert Walpole, but more particularly these in our own times, have occasioned some of the most perfect pieces of writing we have in our tongue. Though, from the nature of the subject, the pieces themselves can scarce exist longer than the dispute which gave them being; yet certainly their effect upon the language will be felt when the quarrel itself is no more, and every thing relating to it forgotten.

Tho' I have affirmed that our language is more perfect now than in any past period—yet there is still much left in it to be corrected.—Indeed there are some defects in all languages, which have crept in by degrees, and are so sanctified by custom, that they can never be corrected. In English there is no difference in writing, tho' there is in pronouncing, the present, and preterperfect tenses of the verbs *read*, and *eat*, and some others. Some unsuccessful attempts have been made to distinguish them by writing *redde* and *ate*. There are more words in Latin of contrary significations which are written the same, than, I believe, in any other language. It is a *defect* if the pronunciation of different words be alike, and a great *fault* if such a pronunciation be the consequence of a refinement. We now pronounce *fore* and *four*, the same; which sometimes makes an odd confusion. "I will come to you at three, I can't come *before*"—and "I will come to you at three, I can't come *by four*"—are pronounced just the same way. This we get by affectedly dropping the *u*. In French *au dessous* and *au dessus* are too much alike for contrary significations. Nature dictates a difference of sound for different meanings: the adverbs of negation and assent, bear no resemblance to each other in any language; and almost all languages agree in some such sound as *no* for denial.

The London dialect is the cause of many improprieties, which, if they were only used in conversation, would not much signify; but as they have begun to make part of our written language, they deserve some animadversion. To mention a few. The custom among the common people of adding an *s* to many words, has, I believe, occasioned its being fixed to some, by writers of rank, who on account of their residence in London did not perceive the impropriety. They speak, and write, *chickens—coals—acquaintances—assistances*, &c. *Chicken* is itself the plural of *chick*, as *oxen* is of *ox*, *kine* (*cowen*) is of *cow*, and many others. *Coal, acquaintance*, being aggregate nouns, admit of no plural termination, nor does *assistance*. If I were to say a bag of shots, or sands, the impropriety would be instantly perceived; and yet one is full as good English as the other. A certain author of great credit, who has taken a strict, nay, a verbal review of the English language, uses them as often as they occur.

As the Londoners speak, so they also write *learn* for *teach*, this is a very old mistake, and occurs frequently in the psalms, *do* for *does* (and the contrary), *set* for *sit*, *see* for *saw*, *tin* for *latten* (which are two different things as well as words), *sulky* for *sullen*, &c. &c. *'Change* and *'sample* have been long admitted denizens.——Even in a dictionary you may find *million* explained to be a fruit well known—as perhaps in a future edition we shall be told that a *fly* signifies a *coach*, and *dilly* a *chaise*.

The London *phraseology* has also been too hard for English. *I got me up*—*he sets him down*—*I got no sleep*—*I slept none*—such a thing is *a* doing—*a* going—*a* coming—*live* lobsters—*live*-cattle—I will call *of* you—do not tell *on* it. All these are writ without scruple. Our modern comedies, and the London news-papers, abound so much in this language, that they are scarce intelligible to one who has never been in the capital. Nay in books for the use of schools, the London dialect is so predominant, that many of the sentences are not to be understood by a country boy, and impossible to be rendered into Latin even by those who do understand them. "I will go and fetch a walk in the Green Park"—"I will go get me my dinner," and such jargon is perpetually occurring.

English has also been corrupted by London *emphasis* and *accent*—I will not tire you by quoting examples, of which a long list might be made to prove the great propensity of the common people to those defects; and would be a farther confirmation of what I just now advanced, that men of learning really commit improprieties, because their ear is familiarized to them.

I have yet something to add on this subject—but I must caution you from imagining that because I find out the faults of others, I pretend to perfection myself. Hogarth says very properly in his Analysis of Beauty, "do not look for good drawing in those examples which I bring of grace and beauty—they are purposely neglected—attend to the precept."

LETTER XII.

I Sometimes provoke you by sporting with what you deem sacred matters. Homer I know is one of your divinities—may I venture to tell you that I never could find that scale of heroes in the Iliad which critics admire as such a beauty?

Hector is supposed in valour superior to all but Achilles—upon what authority? Ajax certainly beat him in the single combat between them; and there are some instances, tho' I cannot recollect the passages, of his inferiority to others of the Greeks.

It is surely a blindness worse than Homerican, not to see many inconsistencies in the Iliad, and it is ridiculous to attempt to make beauties of them. From many which might easily be pointed out, take one or two as they occur to my memory. After describing Mars as the most terrible of beings, and to whom whole armies are as nothing; what *poetical* belief is strong enough to suppose he could be made to retire by Diomed? If Minerva's shield is so vast (the shell of a Kraken, I suppose), can one help wondering why she does not use it as the King of Laputa does his island, when his subjects on Terra-firma rebel? I do not recollect parallel instances in Milton.

LETTER XIII.

YOU have not done me justice—read the memoirs I sent you *properly* before they are condemned:—what is any book if it be not read in that manner by which it may best be understood? A novel, whose merit lies chiefly in the story, should be quickly passed through; for the closer you can bring the several circumstances together, the better. If its merit consists in character and sentiment, it should be read much slower; for the least obvious parts of a character are frequently the most beautiful, and the propriety of a sentiment may easily escape in a hasty perusal. Detached thoughts ought to be dwelt on longer than any other manner of writing; for different subjects following close, do rather confound than instruct; but if we allowed ourselves time to reflect, we should understand the author and perhaps improve ourselves. Each thought should be considered as a text, upon which we ought to make a commentary.

Bayle's manner of writing by text and note is generally decried, but without reason. When there is a necessity of proving the assertion by quotation, which was his case, no other way can be taken equally perspicuous. The authorities must be produced somewhere—they cannot be in the text, and if they are put at the end of the book, which is the modern fashion, how much more troublesome are they for referring to, than by being at the bottom of the page? The truth is, this is another instance of ignorance in the method of reading. Bayle, Harris, and other writers of this class, should have the text read first, which is quickly dispatched; then, begin again and take in the notes. By this means you preserve a connection, and judge of the proofs of what is asserted.

I might in other respects complain of your treating me rather unfairly; indeed, none judge less favourably of an author than his intimate friends——their personal knowledge of him as a man, destroys a hundred delusions to his advantage as an author.—"Who is a hero to his Valet de Chambre?" said the great Condé, and he might have added, "or to his friends?" Besides the obvious reason for this, it is most likely that an author has in his common conversation made his friends acquainted with his sentiments long before they are communicated to the public. The consequence is, that to *them* his work is not new; and it is possible that they may take to themselves part of his merit; for I have known many instances, where a person has been told something by way of information, which he himself told to the informer.

I know you will take this to yourself.—Do so, but still think me

Yours, &c.

LETTER XIV.

WE are got into a custom of mentioning Shakespeare and Jonson together, and many think them of equal merit, tho' in different ways. In my opinion, Jonson is one of the dullest writers I ever read, and his plays, with some few exceptions, the most unentertaining I ever saw. He has some shining passages now and then, but not enough to make up for his deficiencies. Shakespeare, on the contrary, abundantly recompenses for being sometimes low and trifling. One of his commentators much admires his great art in the construction of his verses—I dare say they are very perfect; but it is as much out of my power to think upon the art of verse-making when I am reading this divine poet, as it is to consider of the best way of making fiddle-strings at a concert. I am not master of myself sufficiently to do any thing that requires deliberation: I am taken up like a leaf in a whirlwind, and dropped at Thebes or Athens, as the poet pleases!

I have seldom any pleasure from the representation of Shakespeare's plays, unless it be from some scenes of conversation merely, without passion. The speeches which have any thing violent in the expression, are generally so over-acted as to cease to be the "mirror of nature"—but this was always the case—"Oh! it offends me to the soul, to see a robustious perriwig-pated fellow tear a passion to tatters:"—'tho' this is a "lamentable thing," yet it appears to be without remedy. An actor, in a large theatre, is like a picture hung at a distance, if the touches are delicate, they escape the sight: both must be extravagant to be seen at all, and hence the custom of the ancients to make use of the Persona and Buskin. Acting has a very different effect in the stage-box from what it has in the back of the gallery. In the one, every thing appears rough and rude, like a picture of Spagnolet's near the eye; in the other, it is with difficulty that the play can be made out. Perhaps, the best place is the front of the first gallery; as being sufficiently removed to soften these hardnesses, yet near enough to see and hear with advantage. But there is no place can alter the impropriety of rant and turgid declamation, which the performer naturally runs into by endeavouring to be strong enough to be heard—so that, as I observed, the evil seems to be incurable.

LETTER XV.

AN acquaintance of ours has corresponded with a writing-master many years, not from any regard to the man, but for the pleasure he takes in seeing fine writing. He preserves his letters carefully, and though he *reads* them to none, (perhaps they are still unread by himself) he *shews* them to all who can relish the excellence of a flourish "long drawn out."——Our friend's taste may be ridiculed by those who "hold it a baseness to write fair," but yet it is certain, that the true form of letters, in writing, is understood no where but in England. I never saw a specimen of a correct hand either written or engraved, from any other country, that was upon a right principle. Perhaps it may be objected, that every nation, prejudiced in favour of their own particular manner, will say the same thing. Let us examine this.

Modern writing-hand had its rise from an endeavour to form the true letters as they are printed, with expedition. The first variation from the original, must be an oblique instead of a perpendicular situation, this naturally arises from the position of the hand—the next, a joining of the letters; these two necessarily produce a third, an alteration of the form. So that writing hand differs from printing in this, that the former is an arrangement of *connected* characters, the latter of distinct ones. The slit in the pen makes the down-strokes full, and the up-strokes slight, so that the body of the letter is strong, and the joinings weak; as they should be. It is most natural and easy also to hold the pen always in the same position, by which means, the full and hair-strokes are always in their right places. So far seems the necessary consequence of endeavouring to make the letters expeditiously with a pen. This being granted, the ornamental part comes next to be considered. For this, it is requisite that the letters should be of the same size and distance, that their leaning should be in the same direction, that the joining be as much as possible uniform, and, lastly, that the superadded ornament of flourishing, should be continued in the same position of the pen in which it was first begun, (generally the reverse of the usual way of holding it), and that the forms be distinct, flowing, and graceful.

These appear to me to be the true principles of writing. Examine the Italian and French hands by these rules, (some of the best specimens are the titles of prints, &c.) and the hand which they use will be found to be unconnected, full of unmeaning twists and curlings generally produced by altering the position of the pen, and upon the whole awkward, stiff, and ungraceful.

As they *now* write, we *did*, about seventy or eighty years since; so that our present beautiful hand is a new one, and by its being used no where but in England, I must conclude it to be an English invention.

Believe me, in my best writing, and with my best wishes, ever

Yours, &c.

LETTER XVI.

I Have often reflected with great grief, that there is scarce any remarkable natural object in the sublime style, of which we have a draught, to be depended on. The cataract of Niagara.—The peak of Teneriffe, we know nothing of but that the one is the greatest waterfall, and the other the highest single mountain in the world. It is true, Condamine says, that the Andes far surpass the peak of Teneriffe; more than a third—but, it should be considered, that the valley of Quito is 1600 fathoms above the sea, and that it is from the foot of the mountain that the eye judges of its height. The peak of Teneriffe rises at once, and has, comparatively, but a small base—so that, in appearance, Teneriffe is the highest of mountains. The cataract of Niagara, indeed, is most excellently *described* by Mr. Kalm; but all descriptions of visible objects comes so short of a representation, and is necessarily so imperfect, that if ten different painters were to read Mr. Kalm's account of this amazing fall, and to draw it from his description, we should have as many different draughts as painters. The peak of Teneriffe has been ascended by many, but described by none, for I cannot call those accounts descriptions, which would suit any other high mountain as well. Some travellers give views of what they apprehend to be curious, but all that we can find from them is, that they cannot possibly be like the object described. There must be some amazing scenes in Norway by Pontoppidan's Descriptions, and in the Alps by Schuchtzer's, but their draughts cannot bear the least resemblance to what they describe. Nay, those objects which lie in the common road of travellers have just the same fate.—The view of Lombardy from the Alps—the bay of Naples—the appearance of Genoa, from the sea, &c. &c. are much talked of, but never drawn: or if drawn, not published. From this general censure I should except a view of Vesuvius taken by a pupil of Vernet's, and two views of the Giant's causeway in Ireland, but above all Gaspar Poussin's drawings from Tivoli. These have something so characteristic, that we may be sure that they give a proper idea of the scenes from whence they were taken. Of the many thousands that are constantly going to the East-Indies, not one has published a drawing of the Cape of Good Hope, nor of Adam's peak in Ceylon, nor fifty other remarkable objects which are seen in that voyage.— —Even the rock of Gibraltar is as yet undrawn. What I mean by a drawing is a *pictoresque* view, not a meer outline for the use of navigators, nor the unmeaning marks of a pencil directed by ignorance. I greatly suspect the so much commended draughts in Anson's voyage to be nothing but outlines filled up at random; and more than suspect, that many designs in a late publication of this sort, are mere inventions at home.

I have been led into this subject by the two admirable descriptions of Ætna by Sir W. Hamilton and Brydone—as much as *words* can realize objects, they *are* realized.— But yet, a dozen different views taken by real artists, would have done more in an instant, than any effect within the power of description.

IS there not something very fanciful in the analogy which some people have discovered between the arts? I do not deny the *commune quoddam vinculum,* but would keep the principle within its proper bounds. Poetry and painting, I believe, are only allied to music and to each other; but music, besides having the above-named ladies for sisters, has also astronomy and geometry for brothers, and grammar—for a cousin, at least. I am sure I have left out many of the family, though, if I could enumerate what seems at present the whole, it is odds, but there would be a new relation discovered soon by an adept in this business.—Why should not I find out one or two?—I will try.

Let me see—what is there near me? Oh! a standish—music then shall be like my standish. Any thing else?—Yes—like the grate—or like that shirt now hanging by the fire, which makes so excellent a screen.

"How prove you this in your great wisdom?"

Marry! thus—music bears great analogy to my standish; because there is one bottle for the ink, another for the sand, and the third for wafers—these are evidently the unison, third, and fifth, which make a compleat chord; and those three a compleat standish.—The pen is so evidently the plectrum, that it is insulting you to mention it.

"But why like the grate?"

Bless me! did you never see a testudo,—a lyre? The bars are the strings, the back is the belly—need I enlarge? What is the fire but the vis musica?—and here, the poker is the plectrum.

"But how can it possibly be like the shirt?"

Pho! any thing in analogy is possible.—Like my shirt?—Why, the body is the bass, the sleeves are two trebles—the ruffles are shakes and flourishes—the three buttons of the collar are evidently the common chord.—But, a truce with such nonsense.—There are scarce any two things in the world but may be *made* to resemble each other. Permit me to shew the slightness of another received opinion concerning music.

"What passion cannot music raise or quell?" says Dryden, or Pope, I forget which: and the same thought is so often expressed by other poets, and so generally adopted by all authors upon this subject, that it would be a bold attempt to contradict it, were there not an immediate appeal to general feeling, which I hope is superior to all authority. Thus supported then, I ask in my turn—"What passion *can* music raise or quell?" Who ever felt himself affected, otherwise than with pleasure, at those strains which are supposed to inspire grief—rage—joy—or pity? and this, in a degree, equal to the goodness of the composition and performance. The effect of music, in this instance, is just the same as of poetry. We attend—are pleased—delighted—transported—and when the heart can bear no more, "glow, tremble, and weep." All these are but different degrees of pure *pleasure*. When a poet or musician has produced this last effect, he has attained the utmost in the power of poetry or music. Tears being a general expression of grief, pain, and pity; and music, when in its perfection, producing them, has occasioned the mistake, of its raising the passions of grief, &c. But tears, in fact, are nothing but the mechanical effect of every strong affection of the heart, and produced by all the passions; even joy and rage. It is this effect, and the pleasurable sensation together, which Offian (whether ancient or modern I care not) calls the "joy of grief."——It is this effect, when produced by some grand image, which Dr. Blair, his Critic, styles the "sublime pathetic."

I have chosen to illustrate these observations from poetry rather than from music, because it is more generally understood, and easier to quote—but the principle is equal in both the arts.

Adieu.

LETTER XVIII.

YOUR pictures came safe—my opinion of them you will in part know from the following observations, which, though made on another occasion, are equally applicable to this.

There is in landscape-painting and novel-writing a fault committed by some of the best artists and authors, which is as yet unnamed, because perhaps unnoticed, permit me to call it *a bad association*.

In a landscape, it is not sufficient that all the objects are such as may well be found together.—In a story, it is not enough that the incidents are such as may well happen—it is necessary in both, that all the circumstances should be of the *same family*.

Suppose a landscape had for its subject one of Gaspar Poussin's Views of Tivoli—now, tho' there is nothing more natural than to find mills by running water, yet a mill is not an object that can possibly agree with the other parts of the picture. Suppose in a landscape of Ruysdale there were introduced the ruins of a temple; tho' a temple may be properly placed in a wood near water, yet it does not suit the rustic simplicity of the pictures of this artist.—Give the mill to Ruysdale and the temple to Gaspar—all will be right. These two painters were the most perfect in their different styles that ever existed. Both formed themselves upon the study of nature, both were correct, both excellent; and yet so totally different from each other, that there are scarce any parts of the pictures of one, that will bear being introduced into those of the other. Claude's magnificent ideas frequently betrayed him into *a bad association*.——Large grand masses of trees agree but ill with sea and ships, unless they are removed to a distance.—An English painter, who formed himself upon the study of Gaspar, took his trees, rocks, and other circumstances from that master, but his buildings from the Gardiner's huts at Newington.

A story which proceeds upon a regular circumscribed plan, chiefly consisting of dialogue and sentiment, where the scene is laid in London, and the characters such as are natural to the place; has *a bad association* if the author goes to Africa in quest of adventures. On the other hand, a novel which sets out upon the principle of variety, and where a frequent change of place is necessary to the execution of the design, has *a bad association* if the author in any part of it quits adventure for sentiment or satire. And yet, this has been done by Fielding and Smollet, the two best novel-writers of the age.

END OF THE FIRST VOLUME.

Milton Keynes UK
Ingram Content Group UK Ltd.
UKHW031050120324
439302UK00006B/425